Konnie
the Christmas Cracker Fairy

Join the **Rainbow Magic Reading Challenge!**

Read the story and collect your fairy points to climb the Reading Rainbow at the back of the book.

This book is worth 2 stars.

To Lily Stevenson. Merry Christmas!

Special thanks to
Rachel Elliot

ORCHARD BOOKS

First published in Great Britain in 2020 by The Watts Publishing Group

1 3 5 7 9 10 8 6 4 2

© 2020 Rainbow Magic Limited
© 2020 HIT Entertainment Limited
Illustrations © 2020 The Watts Publishing Group Limited

A CIP catalogue record for this book is available from the British Library.

ISBN 978 1 40835 629 6

Printed and bound in Great Britain by Clays Ltd, Elcograf S.p.A

MIX
Paper from
responsible sources
FSC® C104740

The paper and board used in this book are made from wood from responsible sources

Orchard Books
An imprint of Hachette Children's Group
Part of The Watts Publishing Group Limited
Carmelite House, 50 Victoria Embankment, London EC4Y 0DZ

An Hachette UK Company
www.hachette.co.uk
www.hachettechildrens.co.uk

Konnie
the Christmas
Cracker Fairy

By Daisy Meadows

ORCHARD

www.rainbowmagicbooks.co.uk

Fairyland Palace

Tippington Community Centre

Grand Hotel ↗

Contents

Story One:
The Christmas Candle

Story Two:
The Super Santa Hat

Story Three:
The Glittery Star Earrings

Jack Frost's Spell

On Christmas Day the humans meet
To pull their crackers, drink and eat.
They smile at every joke and hat.
But I will put a stop to that!

Konnie wants to spread delight,
But this year crackers won't be right.
With rubbish jokes and broken toys,
I'll spoil their silly Christmas joys!

Story One
The Christmas Candle

Chapter One
Eco Crackers

"This is going to be great," said Kirsty Tate, smiling at her best friend, Rachel Walker, as they arrived at the Tippington Community Centre.

It was almost Christmas, and Kirsty was staying with Rachel for the weekend. They had tied tinsel into their ponytails, and were feeling fizzy with Christmas excitement.

"It's going to be fun to learn how to make crackers," said Rachel. "Mum said that she'd come and buy some for Christmas Day."

All the crackers were going to be sold at the Tippington Community Centre Christmas Fair that afternoon.

"What will happen to the money we raise at the fair?" Kirsty asked.

"Fingers crossed there will be enough to give the community centre a new coat of paint," said Rachel. "It looks a bit tatty!"

They looked up at the building. It was faded and weather-beaten, and the old paint was starting to peel off. The only thing that made it jolly was the banner hanging above the door, held up with glittering threads of tinsel:

Inside, the room was sparkling with garlands of tinsel. Wooden tables were arranged in a big square and covered with long, red cloths. There were different craft materials on each table. The girls could see bowls filled with cardboard tubes, colourful paper hats, red ribbon and stripy red-and-white string. Lots of people were already bustling around the tables.

A woman hurried towards them, smiling. She had soft, blonde hair that fluffed out around her head like a golden cloud, and a colourful dress with big, orange flowers all over it.

"Welcome!" she exclaimed. "I'm Susie, and I'm running the cracker workshop. What are your names?"

"I'm Rachel and this is Kirsty," said

Rachel, smiling back at her.

Susie took a roll of labels and a felt-tip pen from the nearest table. In a few strokes, she had written their names in beautiful looped writing, decorated with tiny flowers and leaves.

"These look amazing," said Kirsty as she stuck the label to her T-shirt. "Thank you."

Susie led them over to a table where sheets of paper were stacked up in neat piles, covered in printed black writing.

"These are jokes," she said. "I printed them out on my computer at home. All we need to do now is cut each one out, ready to go into the crackers. That's your first job. Just grab a joke sheet and get snipping."

"Will we put the strips of paper into the crackers?" said Kirsty.

"Yes, later," said Susie. "First, we have to get the jokes, hats and eco-friendly gifts ready. Then I'll show everyone how to make the crackers. We're going to have lots of fun being super creative – with no plastic to harm the planet."

Eagerly, Rachel and Kirsty each picked up a sheet.

"Who delivers Christmas presents to cats?" Rachel read out. "Wrap."

She and Kirsty shared a puzzled look.

"I don't get it," said Kirsty.

"Try one from your sheet," said Rachel.

"What do Santa's little helpers learn at school?" Kirsty read aloud. "A puddle."

"That doesn't make sense," said Rachel.

She ran her finger down the jokes on

her sheet and shook her head.

"Not a single one of these jokes is funny," she said. "Something has gone wrong!"

Chapter Two
News from Fairyland

When Rachel and Kirsty told Susie about the jokes, her big smile faded.

"I can't understand how they have been muddled up," she said. "I must have done something wrong when I printed them. Well done for noticing, girls. Oh dear, it's going to take ages to match each joke to the right punchline."

"We can do it," said Rachel in a confident voice. "Don't worry."

"I'll go and tell the other helpers," said Susie.

She hurried over to the next table and Kirsty looked at the pile of joke sheets.

"Oh my goodness, this is a big job," she said. "I wish we had a fairy to help us."

The girls exchanged a little smile, thinking about the marvellous secret that they shared. Since they had first met on Rainspell Island, they had been on countless magical adventures with their fairy friends. Sometimes they had even become fairies themselves.

"Yes," said Rachel with a laugh. "Fairy magic would do this job in a twinkling."

Kirsty started to cut up the jokes on her

sheet, but Rachel noticed a cardboard tube lying under the long curtain at the side of the hall.

"I'll just go and pick that up," she said. "We mustn't waste anything. Every cracker we sell will go towards making the community centre look beautiful again."

She bent down and reached for the tube, but it rolled out away.

"That's funny," she said, going behind the curtain. "Oh my goodness!"

The tube had started fizzing with tiny sparks of coloured light, like crackles of electricity. Rachel popped her head back around the curtain.

"Psst, Kirsty," she whispered. "Come quickly!"

She pulled her best friend behind the heavy curtain and Kirsty gasped.

"It's magic," she said.

There was a little 'POP' and then a tiny fairy shot out of the tube in a burst of green, purple and orange sparks. She landed with a bump and giggled.

"That was a lot of fun," she said, standing up and shaking the last few sparkles from her wings. "I'm definitely travelling like that again. Hello! I'm Konnie the Christmas Cracker Fairy."

Konnie was wearing a swishy red dress

that glittered with stars, and a pair of matching red velvet shoes. Her pixie-cut hair was as golden as the stars on her dress.

"It's great to meet you," said Rachel. "This is Kirsty and I'm Rachel."

"Oh my, I know who you are," said Konnie with another merry giggle. "I came here to find you. Something has happened in Fairyland, and you're the only ones who can help me."

Rachel and Kirsty sat down cross-legged, making sure that they were hidden by the curtain.

"Tell us all about it," said Kirsty.

Konnie's green eyes gleamed as she

began her story.

"It's my job to make sure that crackers give everyone fun, laughter and gifts at their Christmas meal," she explained. "I have three magical objects that help me to do my job. The joyful Christmas candle makes sure that cracker jokes fill every heart with laughter, light and warmth. The super Santa hat keeps each cracker hat looking perfect, and the glittery star earrings make sure that every cracker gift adds extra sparkle to the Christmas meal."

"I love the sound of your job," said Rachel.

"I love it too," said Konnie. "As well as watching over all the crackers in the world, I make a few magical crackers that grant wishes when they are pulled.

I secretly give them to humans who have worked extra hard to spread the magic of Christmas. But yesterday, while I was making this year's crackers, Jack Frost burst into my little toadstool house."

Rachel and Kirsty shared an alarmed glance. They knew how much trouble

Jack Frost liked to cause for the fairies.

"What did he do?" asked Kirsty.

"Hold out your hand," said Konnie. "I'll show you."

Chapter Three
Fishing for Trouble

Konnie tapped her wand on Kirsty's upturned palm, and tiny versions of Jack Frost and Konnie appeared. Jack Frost was pacing up and down, glaring at the little fairy.

"Wow, this is just like watching a play," said Rachel.

"Stop making things for those stupid humans," Jack Frost was saying. "I want you to make one of your magical crackers for me. It has to be the biggest and the best."

"I'm sorry," said tiny Konnie, "but the crackers are only for humans who have done something special for others."

"I don't care!" Jack Frost yelled. "I want one."

"The magic doesn't work like that," said tiny Konnie. "But I will make you some ordinary crackers to share with the goblins if you like."

"Ordinary?" Jack Frost roared. "How dare you suggest something ordinary for me, you stupid fairy?"

"Please don't call me names," said tiny Konnie. "It's Christmas, and I'm trying to

spread a little Christmas joy."

Jack Frost leaned down so that his long, pointy nose was pressed against the fairy's face.

"Christmas is stupid, humans are stupid and you're stupid," he hissed in a scary voice. "I'm going to make sure that no one finds crackers fun this year. By the time I've finished, no human will ever want to pull a cracker again."

He disappeared in a flash of blue lightning. Rachel sat back as the picture of tiny Konnie faded from Kirsty's hand.

"You had a hat and earrings when Jack Frost came to see you, but you're not wearing them now," she said. "Are those your magical objects?"

"Yes, those are the super Santa hat and the glittery star earrings," said Konnie. "And I always keep the joyful Christmas candle in my pocket. But when I woke up this morning, I saw a goblin standing outside my bedroom window. He had pushed a fishing rod through the window and hooked all my magical objects. I zoomed across the room, but I was too slow."

"Jack Frost must have sent him to steal

your things," said Kirsty. "How mean."

"I asked the goblin to give them back, but he just laughed," said Konnie. "He told me that Jack Frost is going to turn crackers into a nasty surprise that will spoil Christmas meals. He's planning mean jokes, horrid plastic presents, broken hats and even empty crackers."

"That's horrible," said Rachel. "Crackers help to make the Christmas meal extra special. If Jack Frost succeeds, everyone will start their meal feeling sad and disappointed."

"We're not going to let that happen," said Kirsty in a determined voice. "Konnie, we want to help."

Konnie clapped her hands and there was another little crackle of orange and purple sparks.

"I'm so glad you said that," she exclaimed. "The other Christmas fairies are busy doing their own jobs, but Giselle the Christmas Ballet Fairy told me that you were sure to be able to help."

"We should go straight to Jack Frost's Castle," said Rachel. "The goblins must have taken the magical objects to him by now."

"Then you're going to need wings," said Konnie with a wink.

Chapter Four
Jack the Joker

Konnie flicked her wand high in the air. A shower of colourful sparks rained down on them, fizzing like tiny fireworks and glittering in their hair and eyelashes. They held hands as they shrank to fairy size and their wings appeared. Swirls of silver and gold dazzled them, and for a moment they could see nothing. Then, with a faint 'POP', they were flung upwards in a burst of purple fairy dust. When the sparkles faded, they saw that they were fluttering outside the grim Ice Castle. Under the grey sky, the towers and battlements were thick with frost.

"Brrr, it's freezing," said Konnie.

With a wave of her wand she gave each of them a warm puffer jacket that shimmered with all the colours of the rainbow.

"Goodness, could it be that Jack Frost is feeling the cold?" said Rachel in surprise. "There's a fire flickering in the throne-room window."

"That's not a fire," said Kirsty, fluttering closer to the window Rachel had pointed out. "It's a candle."

"It's not just any candle," said Konnie with a little squeak of excitement. "That's my joyful Christmas candle."

The fairies flew up to the window and hovered outside. They could hear Jack Frost's raspy voice and lots of squawking goblin laughter. Feeling brave, they peeped in through the window.

Jack Frost was leaning back on his throne. Several goblins were lying on the floor, clutching their stomachs and giggling.

"What do fish sing at Christmas time?" Jack Frost barked. "Christmas corals!"

The goblins hooted with laughter and wiped tears from their eyes.

"What do you get if you cross a pine cone and a polar bear?" Jack Frost demanded. "A fur tree. What says 'Oh! Oh! Oh!'? Santa walking backwards. What did the reindeer hang on her Christmas tree? Hornaments."

The goblins rolled around the floor, hardly able to breathe because they were laughing so hard.

"I've never seen Jack Frost like this before," said Rachel.

"While he has the candle, he controls all the good fun of the cracker jokes," Konnie explained.

"So that's why the cracker jokes at the

community centre don't make sense," said Kirsty. "He's keeping all the laughter to himself."

Konnie gazed longingly at her little candle. It was shaped like a Christmas tree, and it was flickering merrily in the window beside Jack Frost's tattered old curtains.

"If only I could reach through the glass and pick it up," she said. "But one of the goblins will see me. How are we going to get it back?"

"I don't know," said Rachel. "But we had better get it quickly before Jack Frost sets fire to the place. The candle is much too close to the curtains."

Kirsty felt a tingle of excitement flicker down her spine.

"That's how we get the candle back," she said. "Fire!"

Chapter Five
Fire Drill

Quickly, Kirsty explained her plan.

"When we have a fire drill at school, we aren't allowed to take anything with us," she said. "We have to go outside and wait for the fire wardens to count us. If we set off a fire alarm in the castle, everyone will leave the throne room and we can go and take the candle back."

"You're a genius," said Rachel, looking at her best friend admiringly.

"But that means we'll have to go inside the castle," said Konnie in a nervous voice.

"Yes, but don't be scared," said Kirsty. "Rachel and I have done it before. Besides, the candle is next to a window. As soon as we have it, we can open the window and escape."

The fairies flew up to the battlements and down into the courtyard. There were no goblins on guard, because they were all listening to jokes.

"That's the corridor that leads to the throne room," said Kirsty, pointing to a dark archway.

The fairies found a good hiding place

behind a crumbling pillar nearby. Then
Konnie flicked her wand. At once, a loud
alarm blared out, and a voice echoed
around the castle.

"Fire! Fire! This is not a drill. Evacuate the castle. Report to the assembly point in the courtyard. Wait for instructions from the fire wardens. Do not use the lifts."

For a moment, nothing happened. Then

they heard running footsteps. Squawking, squealing and shoving, goblins poured out of the corridor. Jack Frost was there too, sending goblins flying left and right. Konnie flicked her wand again.

"Alert! Fire! This is not a drill!" boomed

the warning voice. "Move away from the corridors. Do not use the lifts. Obey the fire wardens. Evacuate!"

"Now!" whispered Rachel.

The three fairies darted through the archway and zoomed along the damp, dark corridor. In the distance, they heard Jack Frost's voice.

"Hang on a minute," he yelled. "I don't

have any lifts. Or fire wardens. Or a fire alarm!"

"Hurry!" Konnie exclaimed.

Seconds later, they burst into the
throne room. Konnie flew straight to the
glimmering candle. When she picked it
up, it glowed so brightly that Rachel and
Kirsty were dazzled. Konnie blew out

the flame and slipped the candle into her pocket. They could hear the slap-slap of running goblin feet in the corridor.

"Let's get out of here," said Kirsty, flying to the window. "Oh no, the handle won't turn. It's stuck."

"Let me try," said Rachel.

She yanked on the handle but it wouldn't budge. Jack Frost skidded into the room with a gaggle of goblins.

"Get them!" he howled.

"Let's try it together," Konnie cried.

All three fairies heaved on the handle as the goblins charged towards them. *CREEEAK!* The handle turned in the nick of time. Rachel, Kirsty and Konnie tumbled out in a tangle of arms, legs and wings. There was a fizzy flash of orange light, and then Rachel and Kirsty landed

with a bump behind the community
centre curtain. They were human-sized
again. Konnie fell into Rachel's lap.

"We did it!" Kirsty exclaimed.

"Thank you both," said Konnie.

She flew up and placed a tiny butterfly kiss on each girl's cheek.

"I'm going back to Fairyland to check on my special crackers, but I'll be back soon," she said. "We still have two magical objects to find."

"See you soon," said Kirsty.

Konnie vanished in a flurry of crackling sparkles, and the girls shared a happy smile. Then someone pulled the curtain aside. It was Susie.

"What are you two doing behind there?" she asked with a laugh. "You've done a wonderful job with all those jokes."

Surprised, the girls hurried over to their table. All the jokes were neatly cut up and arranged in piles. Rachel looked at them.

"Who delivers Christmas presents to cats?" she read out. "Santa Claws."

She and Kirsty giggled.

"What do Santa's little helpers learn at school?" Kirsty read aloud. "The elf-abet."

"Konnie must have put the jokes right for us," said Rachel. "Hurray! I can't wait to find out what we're going to do next!"

Story Two
The Super Santa Hat

Chapter Six
Unsuitable Stamps

Susie, who was running the cracker workshop, led Rachel and Kirsty to the table covered in brightly coloured paper hats.

"Of course it's wonderful that so many people have turned up to the workshop," she said with a bubbling laugh. "But I'm rushed off my feet!"

"Just show us what you want us to do," said Kirsty. "We're here to help."

Susie handed them an old ice-cream tub.

"This is full of Christmassy stamps and ink pads," she said. "There are all sorts of festive pictures in here. I'd love it if every cracker had a truly unique hat inside. Could you print a special picture on each one? I want them to be perfect."

"No problem," said Rachel, starting to sort through the box. "We want to make every hat look amazing too."

"That's great," said Susie, giving them a warm smile. "Thanks, girls."

She hurried to greet a family who had just walked in. Rachel laid out the ink pads and stamps on the table.

"Let's test them out and see what they are," said Kirsty, pulling a piece of scrap paper towards her.

Rachel used a pink pad to test the first stamp. It was a picture of an Easter egg.

"Oh dear," she said in a dismayed tone.

"That's not right."

"Definitely not," said Kirsty. "Let's try this one."

She chose a yellow ink pad and stamped another picture. Rachel let out a little burst of laughter. It was a dragon breathing the words 'April Fools' Day' out of its mouth.

"That's even worse," she said, and then groaned. "Oh dear. This must be because Konnie's super Santa hat is still missing. Without it, cracker hats will be ruined."

Rachel looked down at the pictures on the scraps of paper.

"Maybe we shouldn't even try to stamp the hats yet," she said. "Something is bound to go wrong, and we can't make them perfect while Jack Frost has the super Santa hat."

Just then, someone called out from the other side of the room.

"Susie, you've given me the wrong stamps," said an older lady in a cross voice. "These are all pictures of kittens."

"My ink pads have all dried out," said

a teenage girl.

Voices of complaint rang around the room.

"These hats are all crumpled."

Susie dashed from table to table, checking the hats and stamps.

"I can't understand it," she kept saying, her forehead wrinkling with worry. "I just can't understand it."

Rachel felt sorry for her. Susie couldn't

possibly know that her workshop was
going wrong because of Jack Frost
and his naughty goblins. She probably
thought it was her fault.

"Susie's tried so hard to set up this
workshop," she said. "I want to find the
missing objects for her as well as for
Konnie."

Just then, Susie rested her hands on their
shoulders and leaned over their table.

"I see you're having trouble too," she
said. "Listen, there's a group of friends
over by the door who are making hats
from scratch. Maybe you would like to
join them?"

"That sounds like fun," said Kirsty.

Susie led them over to where three
boys were sitting, wearing enormous
paper bonnets. Their table was filled with

crowns, top hats, caps and bowlers, all made out of colourful paper.

"These are amazing," said Rachel, bending down to look at them closely. "How did you—"

She broke off as she glanced up at the boys. They were wearing matching green

jumpers. Each had a picture of a sleigh on the front, decorated with jangling icicles instead of sleigh bells. Their faces were half hidden, but Rachel could see long noses and pointy chins. She squeezed Kirsty's hand in alarm.

"Goblins!" she whispered.

Chapter Seven
A Message from Jack Frost

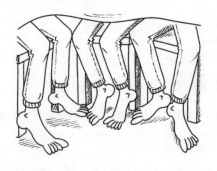

Kirsty bent down as if she were tying her shoelaces and peeped under the table at the boys' feet. Then she straightened up and nodded at Rachel.

"You're right," she said in a low voice. "I'd know those big goblin feet anywhere."

They watched as the goblins worked on more hats.

"There's something unusual about them," said Rachel after a few minutes.

Kirsty nodded. The goblins weren't squabbling or elbowing each other. They were even sharing glue sticks and paper.

"I like your hats," said Rachel.

The goblins ignored her.

"Would you show us how to make them?" Kirsty asked.

"No," snapped the goblin in the pink bonnet, not looking up. "Go away."

"Wow, they're really focused on making hats," said Rachel. "I think they're actually having fun."

The community centre door opened, and Kirsty nudged Rachel.

"I think that's another goblin," she said,

looking at the boy who was walking through the door.

He was wearing a green tracksuit and a cap pulled low over his face. He marched up to the goblins at the table and crossed his arms.

"What are you lot doing?" he hissed.

Rachel and Kirsty took a few steps away from the table, hoping that the goblins would forget about them. After all, they hadn't even looked up from their hats.

"You're meant to be spoiling human hats, not making new ones," said the goblin in the tracksuit. "Jack Frost would explode if he found out. He ordered us to make sure that no human wants to wear a hat on Christmas Day, remember?"

"But these are really awesome hats," said the goblin in the blue bonnet.

He picked up a red paper crown and jammed it on to the new goblin's head. Then he held up a little mirror.

"Wow," said the new goblin, preening himself. "I look amazing."

"Come and help us make more," said the third goblin, whose bonnet was purple.

The new goblin looked longingly at the paper and sequins scattered on the table. Then he shook his head.

"The boss is waiting to hear that humans have gone off cracker hats for

ever," he said. "If we don't get on with it,
he's going to confiscate our bogmallows
for a week."

"Goblins would do anything for
bogmallows," said Kirsty.

Sure enough, the goblins gasped and
jumped up. They hurried out of the
community centre, jostling each other
and squabbling as they went.

"They're back to normal," said Rachel with a sigh. "What are we going to do? We need to tell Konnie that they're here."

"But we don't know where they're going," said Kirsty. "Let's follow them. As soon as they stop, we can find a way to tell Konnie where they are."

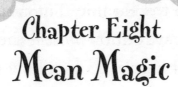

Chapter Eight
Mean Magic

The girls slipped out of the community
centre. It had started to snow, and the
cold little flakes were swirling and
whirling along the pavement.

"There they are," said Rachel.

The goblins were leaning against the
postbox at the top of the street, sniggering

and pointing at the shoppers scurrying
by. Everyone was wrapped up in thick
scarves and woolly hats. Tippington
High Street was at its most festive, with
lots of twinkling lights looped across the
road and sparkling mini Christmas trees
outside every shop.

"We need to get closer so we can hear what the goblins are saying," said Kirsty.

"There's a wall just behind them," said Rachel. "If we sit on the other side of it, we'll be able to hear if they say anything about the magical objects."

They ran up the street, ducked behind the wall and crawled along on their hands and knees. The ground was wet

with melting snow, but it was the perfect hiding place. They could hear everything the goblins said.

"We have to make the humans hate hats," said one squawky voice.

"Put hats on everything," giggled another goblin. "Animals and statues and trees. The humans will be cross that we're making fun of their fashion."

"How do I do that?" wailed a third voice.

"Jack Frost said you have to shake the hat to use its magic," said the fourth goblin.

Rachel and Kirsty exchanged an excited glance. Were they talking about the super Santa hat? Carefully, they peeped over the top of the wall. Yes! The goblin with the purple bonnet

lifted his paper hat. Underneath, he was
wearing a red velvet hat with a white
pom-pom and a furry brim.

"That's why the goblins were so good at making the Christmas cracker hats," Kirsty whispered. "They've got the super Santa hat."

As the girls watched, the goblin wobbled his head wildly and the pom-pom glowed.

POP! A paper hat appeared on a dog walking past with its owner.

POP!

SQUAWK! Two birds were suddenly wearing paper caps.

All along the street, hats appeared on trees, animals and

lampposts. Shoppers pointed at them and started to laugh. The goblins frowned.

"Why are they laughing?" complained the goblin in the green tracksuit. "They're supposed to be cross."

"Look at that cat wearing a hat," said a passing lady. "It's so sweet."

"Stupid humans," grumbled the goblin in the blue bonnet. "They don't know when they're supposed to be annoyed."

Rachel and Kirsty had to stifle their giggles when they saw a snail in a paper hat.

"Think of something else!" the green tracksuit goblin screeched.

The goblin in the magical hat wobbled his head again, and the pom-pom glowed. The woolly hats of the shoppers turned into paper hats, and the wind whisked them away in seconds. People cried out in alarm.

"My hat!"

"It's freezing!"

"Where have all these bits of paper come from?"

In just a few seconds, the road and pavements were littered with all the soggy paper hats.

Chapter Nine
Musical Hats

People darted left and right, trying to find their hats, and slipping on the soggy paper. The snow began to fall more heavily.

"They're Christmas cracker hats!" one man exclaimed. "Yuck, what a mess."

"This is going to take a lot of clearing

up," said a lady.

"Where's my hat?" cried a little boy.

"I hope I never see another cracker hat again in my life!" his mother exclaimed.

Rachel and Kirsty exchanged a worried glance.

"Oh no, the goblins' plan is working," said Kirsty.

At that moment, there was a crackling sound from above. The girls looked up. One of the Christmas lights flickered, and then . . . *POP!* Konnie tumbled out of the light with a fizz and a crackle. Rachel held open her pocket and Konnie landed in it with a bump.

"Oh my!" she exclaimed. "That was a bumpy journey!"

"I'm so glad you're here," said Rachel. "The goblins have turned everyone's winter hats into paper, and they're all getting cross and turning against paper cracker hats."

She let Konnie peep out of her pocket at the sniggering goblins. One of them picked up a paper hat, screwed it into a ball and then hurled it at the goblin in the blue bonnet.

"Hey, that's not fair," wailed the blue bonnet goblin, screwing another soggy paper hat into a ball.

"Oh my," said Konnie. "This isn't the time for games."

"Actually, I think this is the perfect time for games," said Kirsty, smiling. "Konnie, can you disguise us and give us some badges? I've got an idea . . ."

A few seconds later, Rachel and Kirsty strode towards the goblins wearing puffer jackets and thick bobble hats. Konnie was still hiding inside Rachel's pocket.

"Please be careful," she whispered to the girls. "I'm scared of the goblins."

"Hello," said Kirsty in a loud, confident voice. "It looks as if you could do with some help."

"What are you talking about?" said the

green tracksuit goblin rudely. "Who are you?"

Kirsty pointed to the badges that Konnie had magicked up for them.

CHRISTMAS GAMES MONITOR

"We're here to make sure that your Christmas games experience is tip-top," said Rachel in her jolliest tone. "Goodness, are you playing catch with soggy old hats? How old-fashioned."

"We're not old-fashioned," the blue

bonnet goblin squawked. "We're cool."

"All the coolest people are playing musical Christmas hats," said Kirsty. "It's the latest craze."

The goblins exchanged alarmed looks,

and the green tracksuit goblin hid his soggy paper ball behind his back.

"We know that," he snapped. "We were just about to play it. Er, how does it work?"

"We all stand in a circle," said Rachel. "Then we start the music and pass our hats around. If you're not wearing a hat when the music stops, you're out."

"But I don't want to wear anyone else's hat," wailed the goblin who had Konnie's magical super Santa hat.

"Is there a prize?" asked the green tracksuit goblin.

"Er, of course," Kirsty stammered.

The girls exchanged a look of panic.

"Quickly, Konnie," Rachel whispered. "We need something amazing!"

Chapter Ten
Goblin-ball!

Kirsty felt the tingle of magic inside her jacket. She reached into it and took out a magnificent green hat. It was as tall as a wedding cake, decorated with goblin faces, green ribbons and real bogmallow muffins. There was a tiny toy goblin on the very top. The goblins' eyes nearly popped out in amazement.

"Give that to me," demanded the goblin with the super Santa hat.

"First you have to win the game," said Kirsty. "The hat is the winner's prize."

She skipped around to their hiding place, and the goblins followed her. They all sat down in a circle with the green hat in the middle. Konnie waved her wand, and pop music started to play.

"Take off your hat and pass it along," Rachel called out.

She took off her bobble hat and her hair tumbled down. One of the goblins leaned forward to peer at her.

"Do I know you?" he asked.

Rachel's heart thumped. They were surrounded by goblins. What if they were recognised before the hat reached them?

"Keep those hats moving!" she called out.

Slowly, the super Santa hat was moving around the circle towards her. But the suspicious goblin was still staring at her.

The hat was one goblin away when he let out a squawk.

"I do know you!" he exclaimed, clutching the hat to his chest. "Stop the music!"

Rachel dived towards him, and the goblin hurled himself backwards, rolling over and over like a ball. Some snow stuck to him, making him look like a giant green-and-white snowball. That gave Kirsty an idea.

"Snowball fight!" she cried out.

She picked up a handful of snow, rolled it into a ball and threw it at the goblin holding the super Santa hat. *WHUMP!* It exploded against his chest.

"Hey!" he yelled, throwing a snowball back at the girls.

It flew over Rachel's head and the

other goblins jumped up to help him.

"I can distract them," said Konnie.

She waved her wand and a shower of bogmallow muffins landed on the other goblins. They forgot about their friend and started gobbling the yummy treats.

SPLAT! Rachel's snowball hit the

goblin's knees.

"I'm coming for you!" he shouted,
bending down to gather up some snow.

The girls sent another two snowballs
flying towards him.

"It seems a bit unfair," Rachel said,
panting. "There are two
of us and only one of
him."

"I'm better than both
of you put together,"
boasted the goblin. "I
can throw with both
hands at the same time."

He flung his snowballs
at them, but he had
forgotten that he was
still holding the super
Santa hat! It flew

through the air and
Kirsty caught it in
both hands.

"Yes!" she
exclaimed.

Konnie fluttered out
of Rachel's pocket,
her eyes shining. She
touched the hat and
it instantly shrank to
fairy size. The goblin
stamped his foot.

"Rotten tricksy
fairy!" he squawked.
"Not fair!"

"Perhaps I can
make it up to you,"
said Konnie.

She waved her

wand, and a bogmallow muffin appeared in each of the goblin's hands. He stuffed them into his mouth and stomped away, muttering and spluttering cake crumbs.

Rachel and Kirsty peeped into the community centre. Inside, people were

busy stamping Christmas messages on their paper hats. The girls exchanged a happy smile.

"Two magical objects safe, one to go," said Rachel.

"Thank you both so much," said
Konnie, putting her hand over her heart.
"I can give all the shoppers' hats back
now, and I'll be able to do more work on
my special crackers."

"You're going back to Fairyland?"

asked Rachel.

Konnie nodded and waved her wand again. A white cracker appeared in Rachel's hand, twinkling with golden sparkles.

"If you need me, just pull this cracker,"

she said. "Help will come."

"Thanks, Konnie, and goodbye," Kirsty whispered. "I'm sure we'll see you soon!"

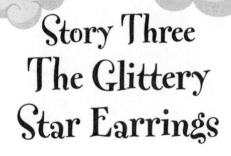

Story Three
The Glittery
Star Earrings

Chapter Eleven
A Whirlpool in the Air

The eco cracker workshop was busier than ever. Susie smiled kindly at them, and Rachel slipped Konnie's magical cracker into her pocket, hoping that she would soon be able to use it.

"It's time for my favourite part of cracker-making," said Susie. "I love putting the little presents inside and imagining all the happy faces when they're open."

She took their hands and led them to a table filled with cracker gifts.

"Fake moustaches, fortune-tellers, mini cards," Susie went on. "Take a cardboard tube, pop one present inside with a hat, a joke and a snapper and then we can wrap the crackers up."

Just then, there was a cry of surprise from one of the people putting the crackers together.

"This moustache is falling apart," he said.

"These hair slides are broken," said a lady beside him.

"It's just like Konnie said," Rachel whispered to Kirsty. "The glittery star earrings add sparkle to every Christmas meal. As long as Jack Frost and the goblins have them, cracker gifts and toys will go wrong."

Kirsty glanced behind her and gasped.

"The goblins have come back," she said.

Two of the goblins were peering at the table of gifts. Rachel and Kirsty tiptoed up behind them.

"I want to go back to Goblin Grotto,"

one of them grumbled. "The Christmas meal is starting soon and the other goblins will steal our crackers if we're late."

The girls exchanged an excited look.

"A goblin Christmas meal with crackers," Kirsty whispered. "I bet that's where we'll find the glittery star earrings."

They ducked under a table and opened their matching necklaces. A tiny pinch of magical sparkles lay inside.

"Just enough fairy dust to transport us to Fairyland," Kirsty whispered.

"Let's find out if it will take us to Goblin Grotto," said Rachel.

The girls felt a delicious tingle of excitement. Soon their fairy wings would be lifting them into the air. What would

their next adventure bring? They drew
in their breath and blew the fairy dust
towards each other . . .

WHOOSH! There was a rush of
sparkles that lifted their hair and caught

in their eyelashes. Gossamer wings unfurled and they shrank to fairy size. At the same time, something that looked like a whirlpool appeared in front of them. It shimmered like water, and when Kirsty reached out her hand, it rippled at her touch.

"Do you think we're meant to go through?" Rachel asked.

They held hands and fluttered forwards. What was waiting for them on the other side of the magical whirlpool?

Chapter Twelve
A Feast in Goblin Grotto

Wherever they were, it was dark and noisy. Bangs, cackles and squawks filled the air. As their eyes got used to the dim light, they saw that they were inside a large wooden hut. There was a long table down the middle of the room, and goblins of all shapes and sizes were squeezed around it. Luckily, it was so dark that none of them had noticed the fairies.

"It's the goblin Christmas meal," Rachel whispered. "The fairy dust brought us exactly where we needed to be."

"Look," said Kirsty, peering through the gloom. "There's a cracker beside every plate."

There was another flurry of loud bangs
as more goblins pulled their crackers.

"Wow, they've got amazing presents,"
said Rachel. "I can see a pair of
binoculars, a compass, even a mini
telescope."

"This is the best Christmas meal ever,"
shouted one of the goblins.

"It's all thanks to that silly Christmas
Cracker Fairy," said another with a mean

laugh.

Kirsty squeezed Rachel's hand hard. "Look at his ear," she exclaimed.

A glittery golden star was dangling from the goblin's right ear. It glowed like a tiny lantern in the gloomy hut.

"I'm sure that's one of Konnie's glittery star earrings," said Rachel. "It's making the cracker presents extra special. But who has the other earring?"

The cheers and cackles of laughter were getting louder. Then a roasted

bogmallow flew through the air and splattered against the wall beside Rachel and Kirsty.

"Food fight!" the goblins shouted.

Seconds later, bogmallows, biscuits, jelly and custard were flying through the air. Rachel and Kirsty ducked down behind a foot-washing trough.

"How naughty to waste all that food," said Rachel.

SPLAT! A cream pie hit one of the goblins in the face. He tumbled backwards off his stool and landed in the foot-washing trough with a loud *SPLASH!* Rachel pressed herself back against the wall, but Kirsty leaned forward. Something gold and sparkling on the goblin's ear had caught her eye.

"He's wearing the other earring," she

whispered. "Maybe I can take it while
he's splashing around."

But as she reached out towards the
goblin's pointy ear, the doors of the hut
crashed open. A spiky silhouette stood
in the doorway, and a blast of icy air
whistled through the room. Suddenly,
every plate, glass and cracker was
bristling with frost. The goblins instantly
fell silent, and Rachel and Kirsty gasped.

"It's Jack Frost," Rachel whispered. "Oh
my goodness, he looks even crosser than
usual."

Jack Frost walked into the room. Icicles
hung from his cloak and made a tinkling
noise as he moved. He glared around the
hut and his gaze sent a shiver down every
spine.

"What do you think you're doing?"

His voice sounded like cracking ice.

"W-we were j-just c-celebrating," said the goblin in the trough.

"Celebrating what?" Jack Frost hissed. "Losing two of the magical items I stole? Fools! Give me the earrings now."

He snapped his fingers, and the

goblin scrambled out of the trough and
squelched towards Jack Frost with the
glittery star earring.

"Oh no," said Kirsty with a groan.
"How are we going to get them back
now?"

A second goblin was shoved forwards,
carrying the other glittery star earring.
Jack Frost took it and closed his fist
around them tightly.

"I'll make sure that Konnie never sees
these things again," he said.

His chilling gaze swept the room again.
For a split second Rachel thought that
his eyes rested on her. But then he spun
on his heel and stalked away, his cloak
whipping around him.

Chapter Thirteen
Ice Statues

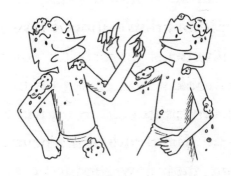

The goblins started to shout at each other.

"It's all your fault!"

"The cracker presents will be spoiled."

"Now we're all in trouble!"

"We have to follow Jack Frost and find out where he's going," said Kirsty.

Staying close to the wall, they crawled towards the door with their wings folded tightly. The goblins were too busy squabbling to notice them. They slipped out into the narrow, snowy street and closed the doors behind them.

"Phew, I don't think anyone noticed us," said Rachel.

"Think again."

The voice was as cold as an iceberg. Rachel and Kirsty shared a fearful glance, and then slowly turned around. Jack Frost was standing behind them.

Rachel and Kirsty gasped and reached for each other's hand.

"I saw the tips of your silly wings poking out from behind the trough," Jack Frost sneered. "You're not going to stop me this time."

He pointed one bony finger at them.
Instantly, ice encased their feet and
ankles, pinning them to the ground.

"That should keep you away from me,"
said Jack Frost.

Rachel looked down at her legs. The

ice was slowly crackling up her shins towards her knees.

"Please wait," she cried out.

Jack Frost hissed like a bitter wind.

"I'm going to spoil Christmas meals in every human town," he said with a spiteful smirk. "Starting with Tippington!"

He vanished in an icy whirl of snow. Rachel and Kirsty looked at each other in alarm.

"I can't pull my feet free," Kirsty exclaimed.

"Nor can I, and my legs are almost completely frozen," said Rachel. "Oh, Kirsty, what are we going to do?"

"Stay calm and think hard," said Kirsty. "We need help."

"I know!" said Rachel, fumbling in her pocket. "Konnie said that help would

come if we used this."

She pulled out Konnie's white cracker, just as her pocket stiffened with ice. The cracker's golden sparkles glittered against the snow.

"Can you reach the other end?" she asked, holding it out to her best friend.

Kirsty leaned forwards as far as she could. The ice had already reached her waist.

"Quickly," Rachel cried. "Before we become ice statues!"

Kirsty managed to grasp the end of the cracker. *SNAP!* There was an explosion of golden fairy dust. When the sparkles cleared, Konnie was fluttering between them.

"Oh my!" she said. "What happened?"

"Please help!" said Rachel. "Jack Frost

has frozen us, and the ice is almost up to my shoulders."

Konnie waved her wand, and a delicious warmth surrounded Rachel and Kirsty.

"It's like being wrapped in a thick blanket," said Kirsty, wiggling her fingers and toes. "Oh, it's so good to be able to

feel my feet again. Thank you, Konnie.
I'm so glad you gave us that magical
cracker!"

"You're welcome," said Konnie. "But
how did you come to be in Goblin
Grotto?"

Quickly, Rachel and Kirsty explained
everything that had happened. When
she heard about Jack Frost taking the
earrings to Tippington, Konnie gasped.

"There's no time to lose," she said. "We
must stop him before he spoils all the
celebrations."

Chapter Fourteen
Jack Frost's Beard

Konnie tapped her wand on the lockets, filling them with fairy dust again. Then she surrounded Rachel and Kirsty with a haze of magical sparkles. Next moment, they were fluttering outside the Tippington Grand Hotel.

"This is where all the early Christmas

meals are being held," said Konnie.

"Why are people having their
Christmas meals before Christmas Day?"
Kirsty asked.

"Lots of workplaces organise a
celebration for all the staff before they
break up for the holiday," Konnie
explained.

A doorman was standing in the hotel
entrance, dressed in a red uniform with
gold buttons. The fairies swooped over his
head and in through the revolving doors.

"I've never been in here before," said
Rachel.

"It's a splendid place," said Konnie, her
green eyes shining. "They do the best
Christmas meals in town. Follow me to
the dining room."

She zipped along a corridor lined

with old paintings. A set of double doors
led into an enormous room with high
ceilings, chandeliers and velvet curtains.
There were several large tables filled with
people.

"I can't see any sign of Jack Frost," said

Kirsty, looking around.

"Let's watch from the chandelier," Konnie suggested. "We can see the whole room from there."

They perched on one of the crystal chandeliers and looked around. The tables looked very festive, with holly, mistletoe and ivy coiling around sparkling goblets and polished silverware. There was a red-and-gold cracker on every plate. Waiters and waitresses glided between the tables, balancing plates of turkey, glazed ham and steaming vegetables.

"I love Christmas meals," said Konnie, clapping her hands and scattering tiny sparkles of fairy dust. "Everyone is so happy and – oh my! Does he look familiar to you?"

She pointed to a waiter with spiky

white hair. Even from above, the fairies recognised him at once. It was Jack Frost!

"I won't let him spoil things," said Konnie in a determined voice.

As fast as an arrow, she zoomed down and tucked herself under Jack Frost's icy beard. Rachel and Kirsty gasped and held their breath, but Jack Frost didn't seem to have noticed.

"That was so risky," said Rachel. "What if he had seen her?"

"She cares more about human beings

than she does about herself," said Kirsty, filled with admiration for Konnie's bravery. "But now she needs our help."

At that moment, some of the customers groaned loudly. They had pulled their crackers and were peering into the tubes with confused expressions.

"I would have thought the Grand Hotel would have better crackers than these," said one man.

"How disappointing," added a lady. "I always look forward to the little cracker surprises."

"Jack Frost must have the earrings with him," said Rachel. "He's using their magic to remove all the presents from the crackers."

"He's not wearing them in his ears," said Kirsty thoughtfully. "Maybe they're in his pocket."

But Rachel shook her head.

"I think they're still in his hand," she said. "Look, his fist is clenched and he's holding it against his chest as if he's keeping it safe."

"Good thinking," said Kirsty. "But how are we going to get him to open his hand?"

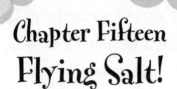

Chapter Fifteen
Flying Salt!

The room rang with the disappointed cries of people who had just pulled their crackers. One man grumpily leaned his elbow on the prongs of a fork, which flew into the air. A waiter caught it expertly and slipped it into his pocket.

"That's it!" Kirsty exclaimed, bouncing

up and down and making the chandelier swing wildly. "We have to take him by surprise and throw something at him. He'll open his hands to catch it, and the earrings will fall down."

"But we can't throw anything at him," asked Rachel. "We're tiny fairies."

"We'll use a fork, just like that man," said Kirsty. "Come on, let's try."

They fluttered to an empty table in the corner and crouched down behind the bottles of water. Together, they dragged a fork into the right position, their hands slipping on the polished silver.

"It feels like trying to move a tree trunk," said Rachel, panting.

Next, they pushed the salt shaker on to the handle of the fork.

"Now all we have to do is jump on

to the other end," said Kirsty. "It should catapult the salt at Jack Frost."

"I wish we could explain to Konnie," said Rachel. "She will have to be speedy to get the earrings when they fall."

"She's clever and quick," said Kirsty. "She can do it. Ready, Rachel? One . . . two . . . three . . . JUMP!"

WHEEE! The salt shaker flew through

the air. Jack Frost didn't notice it. But the well-trained waiters and waitresses spotted it at once.

"Good heavens!" exclaimed the head waiter.

"Catch it!" a waitress cried out.

Jack Frost looked up and saw the salt shaker zooming towards him. His eyes nearly popped out of his head.

"ARGH!" he yelled, throwing up his hands.

He caught the salt shaker and fell over backwards. The girls tried to see what was going on, but they were too far away.

"I didn't see Konnie," said Kirsty.

"Nor did I," said Rachel. "Did she get them? Please let her have got them!"

"I got them," said a happy voice behind

them.

They whirled around, beaming. Konnie was standing with the earrings in her hand. They had already shrunk to fairy size.

"You two are amazing," she said. "What a brilliant idea! I was tucked

under Jack Frost's horrid beard, trying to think of how to get the earrings. When he let them go, I caught them in a flash. Now Christmas meals can be full of fun and sparkle again, and I can finish my special magical crackers."

"And the eco cracker workshop will be a success," added Rachel. "I'm so happy that we could help."

"I'll send you back there in a jiffy," Konnie promised. "Just as soon as we've shared a hug!"

They wrapped their arms around each other. Konnie smelled scrumptiously of gingerbread, cinnamon and spices.

"Thank you," she said, giving each of them a tiny butterfly kiss. "Without your help, there would have been no Christmas crackers this year."

"It was our pleasure," said Rachel.

Konnie smiled, and then waved her wand. When the colourful sparkles faded, Rachel and Kirsty were standing outside the door of the community centre, back to their human size. The door opened and Susie poked her head out.

"There you are," she said. "We've got plenty of wonderful gifts inside our crackers now, but I need help to wrap the crackers in paper and ribbon."

Rachel and Kirsty smiled. Now they could relax and enjoy the workshop.

"By the way," said Susie as they all walked back inside, "did one of you put a special cracker in my bag?"

Rachel and Kirsty shook their heads.

"Well, someone has been very kind," said Susie. "It's the prettiest one I've ever seen, and it sparkles and glimmers like magic. I almost don't like to pull it."

The girls shared a secret smile. They knew that Susie must have earned one of Konnie's magical crackers.

"Don't forget to make a wish when you pull it," said Rachel. "Sometimes, cracker wishes really do come true!"

The End

Now it's time for Kirsty and Rachel to help ...

Elisha the Eid Fairy

Read on for a sneak peek ...

The crescent moon was half hidden behind wispy clouds, the midnight sky glimmered with stars, and Rachel Walker lay asleep in her bed. She was dreaming of her many magical adventures in Fairyland. Most people can only dream of such a thing. But Rachel had often visited Fairyland in real life. Only her best friend, Kirsty Tate, shared the wonderful secret that they were friends with the fairies.

"Rachel!"

The loud whisper broke into Rachel's

dreams. Her eyelids flickered.

"Rachel!" came the whisper again.

Rachel frowned and opened her eyes. It sounded like Kirsty. But how *could* it be? Kirsty was miles away at home in Wetherbury.

"I must have dreamt it," Rachel murmured, closing her eyes and sinking back into sleep.

"Rachel!"

The voice was louder, and this time Rachel felt sure that she hadn't imagined it. She sat up and stared around the room. Who was speaking to her? She crossed her fingers. Please, *please* let this be the start of a new adventure!

"Hello?" she said.

There was an answering patter on the windowpane, like tiny drops of rain.

Rachel jumped out of bed, her heart thudding with excitement. She ran to the window and flung open the curtains. The stars were twinnkling in the sky, and Rachel gasped. Kirsty was outside, fairy-sized, fluttering her gauzy wings against the glass.

Rachel's fingers trembled eagerly as she turned the handle and opened the window. Kirsty slipped inside.

"Brrr, it's cold out there," Kirsty said, rubbing her arms.

She was wearing pyjamas and a dressing gown. Rachel pinched herself to check that she wasn't still dreaming.

"How did you get here?" she asked. "And why are you fairy sized? What's happened?"

Kirsty flew to Rachel's bed and

snuggled under the corner of her blanket.

"I was asleep until about ten minutes ago," she said. "Then I felt something tugging on my earlobe. It was Elisha the Eid Fairy."

"Of course," said Rachel breathlessly. "The new moon is in the sky. Eid will be starting tonight!"

Usually, the fairy adventures that Rachel and Kirsty shared lasted no more than a few days. But their most recent adventures had been very different. Jack Frost and his goblins had stolen the Festival Fairies' magical objects to create his own festival, Frost Day, and now festival days all through the year were in danger of being ruined. The girls had helped the fairies at Diwali and at Hanukkah, but there were two enchanted objects still to find.

"Elisha said that the Festival Fairies needed to talk to us," said Kirsty. "She wanted us to come to Fairyland straight away. She turned me into a fairy and then waved her wand to bring us here to Tippington. But when the sparkles faded, Elisha wasn't with me. Rachel, she's vanished!"

Read **Elisha the Eid Fairy** to find out what adventures are in store for Kirsty and Rachel!

RAINBOW magic

Calling all parents, carers and teachers!
The Rainbow Magic fairies are here to help
your child enter the magical world of reading.
Whatever reading stage they are at, there's
a Rainbow Magic book for everyone!
Here is Lydia the Reading Fairy's guide to
supporting your child's journey at all levels.

Starting Out

Our Rainbow Magic Beginner Readers are perfect for first-time readers who are just beginning to develop reading skills and confidence. Approved by teachers, they contain a full range of educational levelling, as well as lively full-colour illustrations.

Developing Readers

Rainbow Magic Early Readers contain longer stories and wider vocabulary for building stamina and growing confidence. These are adaptations of our most popular Rainbow Magic stories, specially developed for younger readers in conjunction with an Early Years reading consultant, with full-colour illustrations.

Going Solo

The Rainbow Magic chapter books – a mixture of series and one-off specials – contain accessible writing to encourage your child to venture into reading independently. These highly collectible and much-loved magical stories inspire a love of reading to last a lifetime.

www.rainbowmagicbooks.co.uk

"Rainbow Magic got my daughter reading chapter books. Great sparkly covers, cute fairies and traditional stories full of magic that she found impossible to put down" - Mother of Edie (6 years)

"Florence LOVES the Rainbow Magic books. She really enjoys reading now" - Mother of Florence (6 years)

Read along the Reading Rainbow!

Well done – you have completed the book!

This book was worth 2 stars.

See how far you have climbed on the Reading Rainbow opposite.
The more books you read, the more stars you can colour in
and the closer you will be to becoming a Royal Fairy!

Do you want to print your own Reading Rainbow?

1) Go to the Rainbow Magic website

2) Download and print out the poster

3) Colour in a star for every book you finish
and climb the Reading Rainbow

4) For every step up the rainbow,
you can download your very own certificate

There's all this and lots more at
rainbowmagicbooks.co.uk

You'll find activities, stories, a special newsletter
AND you can search for the fairy with your name!